Slugs in Space

D0302186

'Slugs in Space'

An original concept by Lou Treleaven

© Lou Treleaven

Illustrated by David Creighton-Pester

Published by MAVERICK ARTS PUBLISHING LTD

Studio 3A, City Business Centre, 6 Brighton Road,

Horsham, West Sussex, RH13 5BB

© Maverick Arts Publishing Limited May 2019

+44 (0)1403 256941

A CIP catalogue record for this book is available at the British Library.

ISBN 978-1-84886-446-7

www.maverickbooks.co.uk

This book is rated as: Turquoise Band (Guided Reading)

Slugs in Space

by Lou Treleaven

illustrated by
David Creighton-
Pester

Suzy the slug had a very big dream.

She wanted to go into space.

"Why do you want to do that, Suzy?"
asked her mum.

"I want to meet an alien," said Suzy.

"Oh, OK then," said Mum, mashing up
a mushroom. "As long as you're back for
your dinner."

Suzy went outside to look for things for her trip.

First she found an empty snail shell.

"This can be my space suit!"

said Suzy, squeezing into the shell.

Then Suzy found an acorn case.

"This can be my space helmet!" said Suzy,

jamming it on her head.

Finally she found a pine cone. It was

a nice big one.

"This can be my space rocket," she said.

Suzy's friends laughed when they saw her. "Where's the fancy dress party, Suzy?" they said.

Suzy ignored them. "I'm going into space to see an alien," she said proudly.

Her friends laughed even harder.

"Slugs can't go into space!"

"Why not?" Suzy asked.

The other slugs looked at each other.

"They just can't," said one.

"Don't let them upset you, Suzy,"
said Grandpa Sluggins kindly.
"I'm afraid they are right, though.
Slugs can't go into space."

Suzy frowned. "Why not, Grandpa?"

Grandpa Sluggins pointed to a bright light in the sky. "See that? That lamppost is 25 metres away. It would take you 42 minutes to crawl there, if you went at top speed."

"But I don't want to crawl there."

"I know you don't," said Grandpa Sluggins. "But look up at the moon."

Suzy looked up at the white, glowing moon. It was so beautiful. She really wanted to go there.

"The moon is 384,400,000 metres away. It's a lot further than that lamppost. Do you see what I'm getting at?"

Suzy oozed sadly away. Her dream was over,

but she didn't want to give it up just yet.

She wandered on and on, until she found herself amongst rows of neatly planted vegetables. Suddenly a light shone in her face.

"I've caught you, you pesky snail!"

said an angry voice. "Go on, get out of

my vegetable patch."

Before Suzy could move, a huge spade
slid under her.

And then she was flying.

The wind whooshed past her.

Plants and trees went whizzing by until –

SPLAT!

She was stuck in mid air. Something had stopped her moving.

There was a bright light – just like an alien sun. And in front of her was a strange, boxy space craft. There were things floating about in it.

Aliens!

Suzy slid down the window, and landed on soft earth with a PLOP. Then she oozed back home.

When she got there, Grandpa Sluggins
had come to visit.

"Where have you been, Suzy?" said Suzy's
mum. She was just dishing up the dinner.

"Space! I saw loads of aliens – they were the weirdest things ever!" Suzy said happily.

"Well I never!" said Grandpa Sluggins.

"Whatever next?" said Mum.

Tomorrow Suzy would tell her friends.

Then they could all go into space together!

Quiz

1. What is Suzy's big dream?
a) To go to space
b) To travel the world
c) To eat vegetables

2. Why does Suzy want to go to space?
a) To collect cheese from the moon
b) To meet aliens
c) To live on Mars

3. What does Suzy use for her space helmet?
a) A pinecone
b) An empty snail shell
c) An acorn case

4. Where does Suzy land when she goes flying?
a) On the moon
b) On a window
c) In a tree

5. What creatures are the aliens?
a) Fish
b) Slugs
c) People

Turn over for answers

Book Bands for Guided Reading

Pink

Red

Yellow

Blue

Green

Orange

Turquoise

Purple

Gold

White

The Institute of Education book banding system is a scale of colours that reflects the various levels of reading difficulty. The bands are assigned by taking into account the content, the language style, the layout and phonics. Word, phrase and sentence level work is also taken into consideration.

Maverick Early Readers are a bright, attractive range of books covering the pink to white bands. All of these books have been book banded for guided reading to the industry standard and edited by a leading educational consultant.

To view the whole Maverick Readers scheme, visit our website at

www.maverickearlyreaders.com

Or scan the QR code above to view our scheme instantly!

Quiz Answers: 1a, 2b, 3c, 4b, 5a